THE HERO OF CROW'S CROSSING

Anne Schraff

SADDLEBACK
EDUCATIONAL PUBLISHING

red rhino
b OO k s™

Body Switch	**The Hero of**	Sky Watchers
Clan Castles	**Crow's Crossing**	Standing by Emma
The Code	I Am Underdog	Starstruck
Fish Boy	Killer Flood	Stolen Treasure
Flyer	Little Miss Miss	The Soldier
Fight School	The Lost House	Too Many Dogs
The Garden Troll	The Love Mints	Zombies!
Ghost Mountain	Out of Gas	Zuze and the Star
The Gift	Racer	

With more titles on the way …

SADDLEBACK
EDUCATIONAL PUBLISHING
www.sdlback.com

ISBN-13: 978-1-62250-943-0
ISBN-10: 1-62250-943-9
eBook: 978-1-63078-043-2

Printed in Guangzhou, China
NOR/0215/CA21500098

19 18 17 16 15   1 2 3 4 5

MEET THE

Tazmin

Age: 9

Best Part of Crow's Crossing: Lots of things to do outdoors—for free

Favorite Snack: Saltine crackers with honey

Future Goal: College!

Best Quality: Accepts others for who they are

CHARACTERS

MR. RIDLEY

Age: 30½

Worst Habit: Loses his temper a lot

Favorite Book: *The Wind in the Willows*

Little-Known Fact: Wears size 6 EEE shoes for his very short and wide feet

Best Quality: Knows how to inspire people

1
NEW TEACHER

There was no fourth grade teacher at Crow's Crossing School. The fourth graders had to join the third graders. The teacher, Mr. Eckert, was not doing a good job of teaching third grade. Or fourth grade.

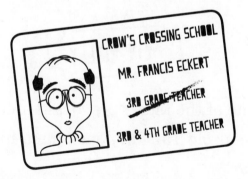

Then Mr. Ridley moved to town. He was hired to teach fourth grade.

Mr. Ridley was a tall young man. About thirty. Thick dark hair. Strange silvery eyes. He looked sad sometimes. And sometimes he looked gray. Like he was scared. Like he had seen a ghost.

MR. RIDLEY

Some of the kids were afraid of him. But nine-year-old Tazmin Jones liked him from the start.

Crow's Crossing was a small town. Most

of the people there had come from bad parts of the city. They were poor. They wanted to get their children out. Because of crime. Because of gangs. And houses were cheap in Crow's Crossing.

"We don't have much here," Mom said. "But we got green hills. We got little streams. Our house is not big. But we got flowers and trees. A great garden."

"I like Crow's Crossing," Tazmin said. "I have friends in school. Mister Ridley is a great teacher. He's the best fourth grade teacher. Maybe ever."

Tazmin's twin brother, Tyree, did not like Mr. Ridley. "He's mean. Crazy. He yells," Tyree said.

"I'm learning," Tazmin said. "I didn't learn from Mister Eckert."

"Well, I'm glad you're learning," Mom said. She quit school. She had to help her mother clean houses. Dad quit school too. Now he did odd jobs in Crow's Crossing.

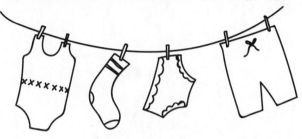

CLEAN OTHER PEOPLE'S CLOTHES? NO THANK YOU!

"I'm getting good at math," Tazmin said proudly. "Mister Ridley helps everybody."

"He gets crazy mad if you don't mind him," Tyree said.

"Not at me," Tazmin said. "*I* mind him."

"We never finished school, your dad and me," Mom said. "That's why we have nothing. But you kids are going to do better. At least we got a clean house. Food on the table."

"And we got the best teacher ever," Tazmin said. She pulled out her paper. There was a gold star on it. Tazmin was so proud.

YOU'RE A STAR

Word had gotten around town. Mr. Ridley was a very good teacher. But everybody wondered why he was here. The pay was low. Nothing was close-by.

Some did not trust him. They thought he was hiding. From someone. Or something.

2
HOMEWORK

The Garners were neighbors. Viv Garner's younger son was Blake. He never got a good grade before. He could barely read. But now he was starting to read simple books. And it was because of Mr. Ridley. Still, Viv wasn't so sure about the new teacher.

BLAKE GARNER'S REPORT CARD

MATH	· · · · · · · · · · · F
READING	· · · · · · · · · · · F
SCIENCE	· · · · · · · · · · · F

"Eve," Viv said to Tazmin's mom. "Why *is* he here? He is so talented. Why Crow's Crossing?"

Eve Jones shook her head. "Maybe he's a good man. Maybe he's a hero. Someone who really cares about kids."

Viv laughed. "I have lived too long to believe that. I'm glad he's teaching my boy to read. But something's wrong with Mister Ridley. He's too good to be true."

"He's teaching Tazmin math. And he's teaching Tyree to read," Eve said. "I'm just thanking the Lord for him. I've had too much bad luck in my life, Viv. I don't look for bugs in every ear of corn."

It was the next morning. Tazmin and Tyree walked to school. "You do your homework, Tyree?" Tazmin asked her brother

"No," Tyree said. "It was about some stupid story. Mister Ridley wanted a whole page. I can't do that."

Tazmin laughed. "I did all my homework. A whole page of math."

"You make me sick," Tyree said. "You want to be teacher's pet."

Tyree grabbed Tazmin's paper. He wanted to rip it. But Tazmin snatched it back. "You watch yourself, Tyree. Behave. Or I'll tell on you."

The twins caught up to Blake Garner. He was smiling. "I finished my reading homework," he said. "Mister Ridley is good. But why's he here? Maybe he's hiding out from the cops. Maybe he's a criminal. Or worse. My mom doesn't trust him."

Homework was turned in first thing. It was Mr. Ridley's rule. He had a tray on his desk for it. Tazmin marched up. Some kids followed her. She put her work in the tray.

"Okay," Mr. Ridley said. "No homework. No recess. Spend that time studying. You know who you are." Mr. Ridley's silvery eyes looked on fire.

Tazmin really liked him. But he looked scary. His wild black hair seemed to stand straight up.

Crow's Crossing School was poor. There were no computers. Teachers still wrote on chalkboards. They felt lucky to have desks. Some in the county wished the poor people in Crow's Crossing would move. Then they could close the old school.

But the little school meant hope. Maybe the only hope for a poor kid. It was important to the Joneses. And the Garners. And many others in town. They wanted their kids to succeed.

Mr. Ridley came to Tyree's desk. "Tyree Jones," he shouted. "Tell me why you hate yourself so much."

Tyree glared at the teacher. "I don't hate myself. I hate you!" he yelled back.

There was a gasp. The students were shocked. But not Mr. Ridley. "Know what, Tyree?" he said. "*You* want to end up in the gutter. *I* want you to get a good job. A nice car. *You* want to be homeless. And hungry. *I* want you to live in a nice place. Eat good food. Have a good life. So who really hates Tyree Jones? You or me?"

"I can't read that stupid book. No way,"
Tyree said. "I'm stupid. Okay?"

"Never say that. Ever. Nobody says
stupid in this room!" Mr. Ridley looked mad.
"No recess, Tyree. You and I will be inside.
Working on your reading. You will find out
you're not stupid," Mr. Ridley said. "Nobody
in this school is stupid."

3
NO RECESS

It was recess. Tazmin and Blake were playing on the monkey bars. It was not much fun. The bars were rusty. So instead, Tazmin and Blake sat on a rock. They talked.

"You know what my mom noticed?" Blake

RUSTY

said. "Mister Ridley's fingernails. They're broken. Cracked. Mom says he's doing other stuff. Not just teaching."

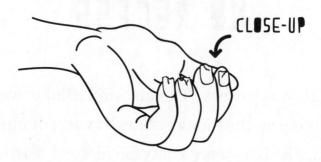

CLOSE-UP

"Who cares?" Tazmin said. "Lots of men like to garden. Dig in the dirt. Mess with cars. Stuff like that."

Just then May sat down. May Steele was Tazmin's best friend. May's mother was a nurse. The Steeles lived in one of the nicer homes in town. May was smart. She even got good grades when Mr. Eckert taught.

"Some kids are talking," May said. "They're saying it's weird. Why would

Mister Ridley come to Crow's Crossing? He can make more money at other schools. He's too good."

"That's what I hear too," said Blake. "Maybe he is hiding something."

"My mom could make more money. But she would have to work in the city," May said. "She wants to help people here. Some people are like that."

"Yeah," Tazmin said. "I think Mister Ridley is like that. I just love him so much. He's like a hero. He wants to do good."

School was over. The kids watched Mr. Ridley leave. He drove a beat-up truck.

"I wonder where he lives," Tazmin said.

"On Shadow Hill," May said. "We saw him one day. He drove into the hills. A trailer was there."

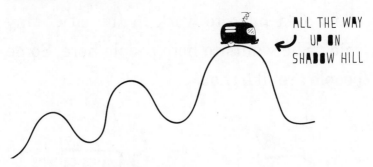

ALL THE WAY UP ON SHADOW HILL

Tazmin shivered. What a wonderful hero Mr. Ridley was. He could make good money in the city. But no. He was here. In Crow's Crossing. Helping poor kids. And he lived in an old trailer! The pay must be bad.

The twins walked home.

WALKING HOME

It was time for homework. Tyree struggled with his work. He asked his parents lots of questions. But they couldn't help. Dad couldn't read. Mom could. But barely.

"What's this word?" Tyree groaned. "C-o-n—"

Tazmin looked over her brother's shoulder. "That word is *confidence*. It means you think you can do something," she said.

Tyree glared at his sister. "You're Miss Smarty-Pants. I don't need you teaching me."

"I was just trying to help," Tazmin said.

Tyree sighed. "You can help. But only if I say so," Tyree said. "Okay?"

Tazmin and Tyree worked together. Then it was time for dinner. Tyree said something to Tazmin. It sounded like *thanks*.

4
GOSSIP

Weeks passed. But the gossip didn't stop. The whole town was interested.

Tazmin talked to her mom. She told her what kids were saying. About Mr. Ridley hiding something. Something bad. Maybe criminal.

"Well, I don't care much about it. Here's

what I know. Mister Ridley is helping you kids. The man is a hero in my eyes," Mom said. "I don't know where he came from. Or why. But I'm glad he's here. That's all I can say."

The doorbell rang. It was Blake. He was excited. He had big news. It was about Mr. Ridley. "My dad and his friend were hunting last night. Guess where? Shadow Hill! Guess who they saw?"

"No clue. Big Foot?" Tazmin giggled.

"No," Blake said. "Mister Ridley was out there. It was around midnight. He was digging like crazy. Had a big shovel. Looked nuts with that wild hair. It was sticking up all over"

"Mister Ridley was probably clearing weeds," Tazmin said. "Go away, Blake. It's late. Don't you have homework?"

Blake left. Then Tazmin called May. "That Blake. He's nosy. Mister Ridley is helping him so much." She talked about Blake's visit.

"Yeah," May agreed. "Mister Ridley has muscles. He has to stay in shape. Maybe he was exercising."

"Hm," Tazmin agreed. "Oh, May. A call is coming through. I have to go. See you tomorrow!"

"Okay. Bye," said May.

"Hello," Tazmin answered.

"Hi, Tazmin. It's Mrs. Garner. Let me talk to your mom."

Tazmin's mom got on the line. But Tazmin didn't hang up. She listened. She knew it was wrong. She couldn't help it. The Garners were gossips.

"My husband said Mister Ridley was digging. Like a crazy person. Maybe he was burying something. Ooh. Evidence! A body? Gives me the creeps, Eve."

"You ever hear of m-y-o-b, Viv?" Mom said. She was mad.

"Yeah. It's mind your own business. But, Eve. This man is teaching our kids. If there's something wrong with him? Well, we need to know."

"Now, Viv. The kids say he's great. He is helping them. Helping all the students. Going from desk to desk. Tazmin's so much better at math. Mister Ridley is teaching

Tyree to read. A whole book! Imagine that,"
Mom said. "And Tyree did his homework."

"Well," Viv said. "I like what Mister
Ridley has done for Blake too. But we need
to be careful. We need to watch him."

"Watch yourself, Viv. You're poking your
nose where it does not belong," Mom said.
"Instead of cleaning. Instead of cooking."

Viv Garner fussed. Then she hung up.

"Some people have too much time," Mom
grumbled.

Tazmin hoped Viv Garner would not talk to anyone else. Especially not the principal of Crow's Crossing School.

Old Ms. Davis was the principal. She used to teach sixth grade. But she wasn't good. So she became principal. She wasn't much of a leader. Tazmin thought Ms. Davis needed a little more courage. To stand up to the town gossips. To fight for the kids.

Tazmin hoped Mrs. Garner didn't cause trouble.

5
PRINCIPAL'S VISIT

It was the next morning. Before class, Tazmin and May made a plan. They got some kids to write the principal. They wrote little notes about Mr. Ridley. About how great he was. How much they liked him.

MR. RIDLEY IS SO AWESOME

They weren't sure it helped. Mrs. Garner must have called. Because Ms. Davis came into the classroom. She wanted to check him out. So she watched. And listened.

Ms. Davis looked very serious. She sat in the back of the room.

MS. DAVIS

Mr. Ridley looked surprised. His silvery eyes flashed. He brushed his hair off his face. He smiled. "Welcome to our classroom, Ms. Davis. This is delightful. A surprise," he said.

Tazmin was scared for him. She hoped he wouldn't get nervous. Mess up. But Mr.

Ridley carried on. Same as usual. He split the class. One reading group. One math group. He gave each work.

Then he moved between the groups. Checked their papers. Gave advice. He looked like a wizard. He was working magic. He laughed with kids. He softly corrected some.

One boy struggled to say a tough word. Mr. Ridley went to the board. Wrote the name of a country.

UNITED STATES OF AMERICA

Afghanistan

"Class. Look up here. Can someone pronounce this word?" the teacher asked.

A girl raised her hand. She pronounced it right. Mr. Ridley looked pleased.

"Does anyone know where this country is?' he asked.

"Africa?" a boy said.

Mr. Ridley stood at the dusty blackboard. Shook his head. "No," he said. "Wrong continent. Let's try again. Anybody else?"

May raised her hand. "It's in Asia. It's between Iran. And Pakistan," she said.

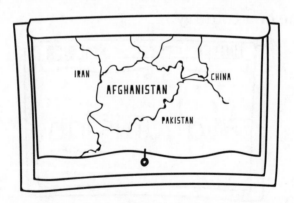

Mr. Ridley's eyes widened. "Very good! How do you know that, May?" he asked.

"My mom was in the war there," May said. "She was a nurse with the army."

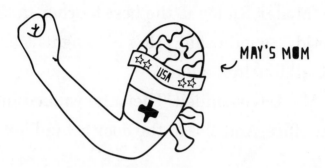

MAY'S MOM

Mr. Ridley pulled down a worn map. He pointed to Afghanistan. "Here is where I was," he said. "Kandahar. My two best friends died there."

There was silence in the room. Then the bell rang. Ms. Davis walked to Mr. Ridley. She thanked him for letting her visit. No one could tell if she was happy.

Later, Tazmin saw the principal. "Ms. Davis," she asked, "did you get the notes we wrote you? The ones about Mister Ridley."

"Yes, I did. They were very nice," Ms. Davis said.

"Mister Ridley is the best teacher in the world," Tazmin said. "He's helping us learn. We all like him a lot."

Ms. Davis smiled. Then she walked into her office. And closed the door behind her.

Word spread around town. Everyone talked about the teacher. About being seen on Shadow Hill. Digging.

Blake had an older brother, Monte. He was in sixth grade. But he could barely read. He liked to skip school. He played hooky with his friend Jasante. Sometimes they got into trouble.

Blake bragged to Tazmin. Monte was going to spy on Mr. Ridley. He was taking Jasante.

"They're going to find out what's up," Blake said. "They're going to Shadow Hill. Mister Ridley will probably be digging again. They'll find out what's what."

SPY GEAR

"Why don't you leave our teacher alone?" Tazmin cried.

"Chill out," Blake said. "Don't you want to know?"

Tazmin turned away. She ran home. She had to tell her dad. Those boys were no good. Spying on Mr. Ridley. Going to Shadow Hill. Maybe her dad could help.

6
SHADOW HILL

Tazmin told her dad about the boys. Mr. Jones listened to his daughter.

"Hm. Well, when those boys take off on their bikes? Look out! 'Cause somebody might be following them." Dad winked at Tazmin. "Keep them out of trouble."

MONTE   JASANTE

NO-GOOD 6TH GRADE TROUBLEMAKERS

Tazmin threw her arms around her dad. "You always know what to do, Dad," she cried.

Dad grinned. "I am proud of you," he said. "Keep working hard. Keep learning."

Mr. Jones knew the hills around Crow's Crossing. He waited by the Garners's house. Behind some trees. Then Monte and Jasante came out. They jumped on their bikes. And headed in the direction of Shadow Hill.

MONTE   JASANTE

Mr. Jones was right behind them. They had reached Shadow Hill. Tazmin's dad could see a man digging. He didn't seem quite right. What was going on?

Mr. Jones didn't know Mr. Ridley well. But the man with the shovel *was* the teacher. He was easy to recognize. Even after dark.

The boys got off their bikes. They moved toward Mr. Ridley. Dad got off his bike. He hid behind a rock.

"Hey! Is that you, Mister Ridley?" Monte yelled. "Why you out late?"

Jasante shouted, "What you doing, Mister Ridley?" Both boys were laughing.

Mr. Ridley stood up. The moon was rising. Even from a distance, the teacher looked angry.

"Get off this land," Mr. Ridley roared. "Get off my land."

"This land don't belong to nobody," Monte said.

"It's mine," Mr. Ridley shouted. "See my trailer over there? I live here. This is *my* land. Now go away!"

"You burying something? You crazy?" Jasante teased.

Mr. Jones looked at the ground. He noticed a few holes. They seemed fresh. Like Mr. Ridley just made them. Some were shallow. Some had been filled back up. Mr. Ridley came at the boys.

Mr. Jones decided to act. He was a big

man. Powerful. "You boys, Monte and Jasante," he yelled. "Do your folks know where you are? Hm. I don't think so. When they find out, you will get it. Big-time trouble. Go home! Now! Or I'm telling them. Scram!"

Both kids got on their bikes. And took off. Mr. Jones came closer to Mr. Ridley.

"You're Tazmin and Tyree's dad," Mr. Ridley said. "How did you know to come here?"

"Tazmin overheard those boys. Said they were coming here," Dad said. "Troublemakers, the two of them."

"Well, maybe you're curious, Mister Jones. About what I'm doing," Mr. Ridley said. "Wouldn't blame you."

"I'm no snoop. That's your business, Mister Ridley."

"I appreciate that," Mr. Ridley said. "But I'm looking for water. For a well."

"Uh-huh." Mr. Jones smiled. He didn't believe the teacher's story.

7
INVITATION

It was the next morning. The family ate breakfast. Dad told them what happened. But he did not share his thoughts. He didn't say that Mr. Ridley was lying.

SPOOKY S

BREAKFAST OF CHAMPS AND HEROES

"I scared those boys good. They took off fast," Dad said.

Tazmin hugged her father. "You're my hero," she said.

"Speaking of heroes," Mom said. "Tazmin said Mister Ridley served in the army. In Afghanistan. Two of his friends died there. Living alone, I'd bet he doesn't cook."

OVEN NOT USED FOR COOKING!

Mrs. Jones smiled at Tazmin. "He'd love a home-cooked meal. Why don't you ask him over? Maybe for dinner this Sunday. We got fried chicken. Sweet potato pie."

"Oh, Mom," Tazmin cried. "Can I really ask him?"

"He probably won't come," Tyree said. "He's helping me a lot. But I still think he's weird."

"Well, Mister Ridley is probably sad. And scared. That war was a bad one. And he lost two friends. He served our country," Mom said. "Now he's helping Crow's Crossing. Teaching our kids. It's the least we can do. So invite him to a chicken dinner."

CLINK!

"I'll ask him," Tazmin said. "And I'll bet he comes."

"Bet you not," said Tyree. "I'll bet you a

chocolate sundae. He won't come. He doesn't want to sit at our table."

"You're on," Tazmin said. But she wasn't so sure herself.

At school, Tazmin placed her homework in the tray. She was always first to do that. Mr. Ridley was sitting at his desk. He smiled. "Thank you, Tazmin," he said.

Now was the time to ask. Tazmin's knees went weak. They were alone. If he said no, nobody would hear. Nobody would tease her. She stood by his desk. Silent.

"Yes, Tazmin?" Mr. Ridley asked. "What is it?"

"My mom. Um. She wants to know ... Sunday dinner. Can you come? I mean ... to our house," Tazmin said quickly. "This Sunday. Mom is a good cook. We'd be proud to have you, sir. We eat dinner at one. It would be cool if you came." Tazmin's voice squeaked. Her heart pounded. She was nervous.

Then, silence. Mr. Ridley was quiet. "Why that's very kind of your mother, Tazmin," Mr. Ridley said.

Tazmin knew what was coming next. Her heart sank. He was going to say no.

"Our house is the green one. At the corner of Aspen and Oak. You can't miss it. We got a big oak tree in the front," she blurted.

"Yes. I've seen your house," Mr. Ridley

47

said. "I would be happy to come for Sunday dinner. Tell your mother thanks. So nice of her."

Tazmin was shocked. She didn't believe what she'd just heard. Then she realized he'd said yes. She smiled. "You'll love Mom's fried chicken. It's the best ever," she said.

The other kids came into the classroom. They just beat the bell. Being late meant missing recess. Tyree looked at his sister. He could tell he lost the bet.

LOOKS LIKE TYREE OWES ONE OF THESE!

Tazmin did not tell any kids that Mr.

Ridley was coming. She didn't even tell May. She didn't want anything to spoil it.

Mr. Ridley! With his silvery eyes. And his thick black hair. He was coming to her house! Mr. Ridley. Tazmin's hero. The best teacher in the world.

8
SUNDAY DINNER

Sunday came fast. Mom found sunflowers to put on the table. She ironed the white tablecloth. It had yellow daisies around the edges.

"You think it looks nice enough?" Mom asked.

Dad laughed. "Don't worry. That man lives in an old trailer. He's regular folk. Like us."

"Oh, Mom," Tazmin said. "The chicken smells so good. And the salad looks yummy."

Tyree still couldn't believe his teacher was coming. "Maybe he just said he's coming. But not really," Tyree said.

Ten minutes before one, Mr. Ridley pulled up. He was in his rusty truck. It was easy to hear on the gravel driveway.

"He's here, Mom," Tazmin screamed.

Mr. Ridley shook hands with Tazmin's parents. He greeted Tazmin and Tyree. Then took his place at the table.

"You want to say grace, Mister Ridley?" Mom asked.

"Please, do it for all of us," Mr. Ridley replied.

The Joneses were not nosy people. They didn't ask Mr. Ridley any personal questions.

Mr. Ridley praised Mrs. Jones's food. The fried chicken was great. Her homegrown tomatoes were the best.

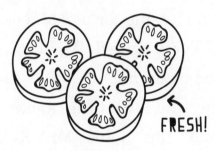

FRESH!

Then he said, "I taught in Los Angeles last year. They did not renew my contract."

"I understand there were a lot of cutbacks," Dad said.

"Yes, sir," Mr. Ridley said.

There was a nervous silence around the table.

"I was just home from the war. I was

messed up," he explained. "I needed a new setting. I remembered my grandfather. He had a little piece of land. Right here in Crow's Crossing. But how would I make a living? Then I got lucky. There was an opening at your school."

"What a blessing for us," Mom said.

"Yeah," Tyree agreed. "Mister Eckert was bad. Called us dumb."

Nobody said anything about Shadow Hill. About the holes Mr. Ridley was digging. And Mr. Ridley didn't mention them.

The teacher thanked them for the meal. Then he said good-bye.

9
LEAVING?

Tazmin was so happy. School was going well. Kids were happy. Everyone was learning.

One day Tazmin overheard Mr. Ridley talking to another teacher.

"I envy you," Ms. Weems said. "You are

such a great teacher. I think it's a gift. You have it. Or you don't."

"Well, thanks. But I don't know about that," Mr. Ridley said. "I will be leaving. Soon. After the holidays."

No! Tazmin felt crushed. Like a rock fell on her. She ducked into a corner. She kept listening.

"Oh! That's too bad," Ms. Weems said.

"You have been so great with the kids. What a loss for our school."

"I wanted to make a difference. Then the war. I wanted to help. People were suffering. But all I got was a messed-up head. And lots of grief. My buddies were killed. My best friends."

Ms. Weems nodded.

Mr. Ridley took a deep breath. "I just came into a lot of money. Now I can go back to L.A. Live the good life. It's what I want."

"Well, I wish you luck," Ms. Weems said sadly. "But the students will miss you. We all will. You taught all of us. You made us better."

Tazmin was near tears. She could not believe it. She didn't want to. She watched Mr. Ridley walk back to class.

The teacher was Tazmin's hero. He came

to a broken school. In rundown Crow's Crossing. He wanted to help poor kids. Kids who had little chance of making it.

Mr. Ridley was changing lives. But now he was leaving. That's not what heroes did.

Tazmin made a plan. She talked it over with the other kids.

"He means so much to us. What if we told him how much?" Tazmin said. "Tyree can read. I can do math. Heroes don't leave."

"I'm with Tazmin," Tyree said. "Who's with us?"

All the fourth graders nodded. They were in.

It was the day before the holiday break. The sun was shining. The air was crisp. There was snow on the hills.

The kids agreed. Tazmin would talk. They would stand behind her. They would do it after school.

The day dragged on. Tazmin was all nerves. Then the final bell rang.

Nobody moved.

"Class dismissed," Mr. Ridley said.

Still nobody moved. Tazmin was scared. She blinked. Cleared her throat.

"Class?" Mr. Ridley said.

"I heard a rumor. You might be leaving us, Mister Ridley. I hope it isn't true," Tazmin said.

Mr. Ridley said nothing. He sighed. He squirmed. Then he stood. "I didn't come here to teach. I came to look for something."

The kids stared at him.

"My grandfather had gold. A lot of gold. He didn't trust banks. So he buried it. You all know where by now. Shadow Hill. Well, I found it. I dug it up. And now I'm rich."

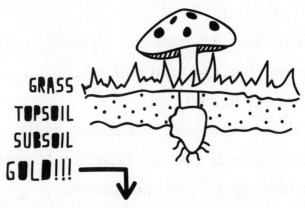

GRASS
TOPSOIL
SUBSOIL
GOLD!!!

"So you don't need a job," Tyree said. "You're giving up on us."

"But, Mister Ridley," May sniffed. "You are the best teacher. The best ever."

"Yeah!" said Blake. "I even like school now."

Tazmin looked at Mr. Ridley. "We all love you. I'm good at math. Tyree is reading books. Blake is too. May is smarter than ever."

"Are we just a job? Are we?" May asked.

"We're poor. We don't have lots of things," Tazmin said. "But we have you! The rest doesn't matter. Please! Please don't leave us." Tears ran down her face.

Mr. Ridley looked sad.

"Class is dismissed. Please clear the room," he said. "I'm sorry, kids. So ... sorry."

Then he ran from the classroom.

"Heroes don't run away," Tyree yelled.

The kids all stood together. Nobody could think of anything to say.

10
HEROES

The holidays were not a happy time. Tazmin and Tyree loved Christmas. Not this year. They knew when school started Mr. Ridley would be gone. Long gone.

RUINED CHRISTMAS

On the first day back, Tazmin and May walked together. Tyree walked with Blake. They saw their school It looked different.

Rotting wood had been replaced. Windows had been washed.

Tazmin peeked inside a classroom. New desks? Was this their school?

Who would teach fourth grade now?

They walked into their classroom. Mr. Ridley? There he was! Waiting for the bell to ring.

The kids started talking. And laughing. All at the same time.

"Take your seats, boys and girls," the teacher said calmly. "Settle down. Today we're going to talk about history."

Tazmin couldn't stand it. She raised her hand. Waved it wildly.

"Yes, Tazmin," Mr. Ridley said.

"But you were supposed to be gone. And you're here! What happened? Tell us. Please."

The other kids nodded their heads.

"I thought one thing would make me happy. But I was wrong. You kids make me happy. Teaching you. Helping Crow's Crossing School," Mr. Ridley said.

"New desks?" Blake asked. "What's that white screen up there? School board feeling generous?"

The kids murmured.

"Ah. It's true. The school has a new look.

65

I guess we just got lucky. Now let's begin our history lesson," Mr. Ridley ordered.

To Tazmin, the new stuff was nice. But having her beloved teacher return? That was priceless.

It was the end of the school year. The shabby school was fixed. It was painted. Laptops appeared. There were new books.

The playground had new monkey bars. New slides. New swings. New grass.

Some teachers left. New teachers came. A librarian was hired.

There were some familiar faces in sixth grade. A couple months ago Monte and Jasante returned. Nobody could believe it. They had been written off.

People talked. Where did the money come from?

Mr. Ridley was living in town now. He sold his trailer. Bought a small house.

The teacher gave a speech to his class. Next year he would teach fifth grade.

All the kids cheered. Even Tyree. Even Blake. Mr. Ridley stood. Each kid came up to give him a high five.

HIGH
FIVE!

Fifteen years later. Tazmin was getting ready for school. This time she was the teacher! Her first job. And she was working at her old school.

Crow's Crossing School had changed. It was larger. Kids came from around the county. The school had the best test scores in the state. Everyone wanted to teach here. Tazmin felt lucky.

She walked into the principal's office. She waited. Looked around. There were pictures of two kids on the principal's desk. And another. A smiling family of four. The parents looked happy.

"Tazmin! Welcome home," Mr. Ridley said. His hair was still wild. His eyes still silver. But he looked calm. And content. The sadness was gone.

"Principal Ridley," Tazmin said, turning. She shook Mr. Ridley's hand. "Thank you for hiring me. I won't let you down, sir."

"I know you won't, Miss Jones." Mr. Ridley smiled. "You have a special boy in your fourth grade class. My son, Alex. He loves math. Just like you did. But watch out for his mother," Mr. Ridley said with a laugh. "She's president of the PTA. And quite a handful."

"We'll get along just fine," Tazmin said. "My room is ready. I can't wait to meet the kids. Um … Mister Ridley? I have to say something … thank you. Thank you for changing our school. Our lives."

"Taz—" Mr. Ridley started.

"I know you used your gold," Tazmin

interrupted. "For us. You could have gone to L.A. Never worked another day. But you stayed. You are a hero. To me. To this town."

"You saved a sad man. A little nine-year-old girl. I stayed for you. For Tyree. For the other kids." Mr. Ridley looked out the window. "But I also stayed for me. I needed to. Being here is what made me whole again."

"I am excited to give back," Tazmin said.

"You will do great. Now get to your class! You don't want to be late on your first day."

Tazmin shook the principal's hand. She turned to leave.

"Tazmin?" Mr. Ridley said. "*You* are the real hero of Crow's Crossing."